ISBN 978-0-98181264-9

15 14

Published by
Ampersand, Inc.
1050 N. State Street
Chicago, IL 60610
www.ampersandworks.com

Printed in Canada

We love our city. But it was our children who inspired us to write and illustrate this book. Our hope is that other parents will find time at the end of a busy day to read with their children and talk about things that make New Orleans so unique.

For our girls:
Christen
Kay
Bailey
Marissa
Rachel
Corinne

Goodnight red beans, goodnight rice

Goodnight pralines and Zatarain's spice

Goodnight cathedral, goodnight French Quarter

Goodnight Café Du Monde

Goodnight Muddy Water

Goodnight po' boys and Hubig's pies,
Goodnight Lucky Dogs and Cooter's fries

Goodnight to the Saints
and the Dome filled with noise.

Goodnight to the fans
cheering "Bless you, boys!"

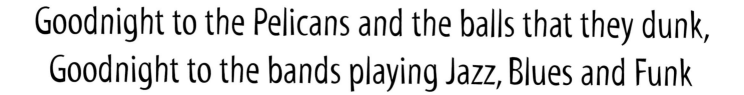

Goodnight to the Pelicans and the balls that they dunk,
Goodnight to the bands playing Jazz, Blues and Funk

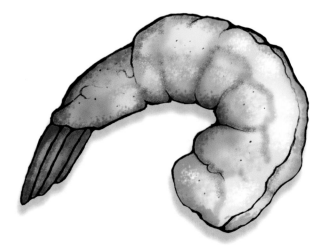

Goodnight to the restaurants with their glitz and glam,
Goodnight to the cooks and to chefs who yell,"BAM!"

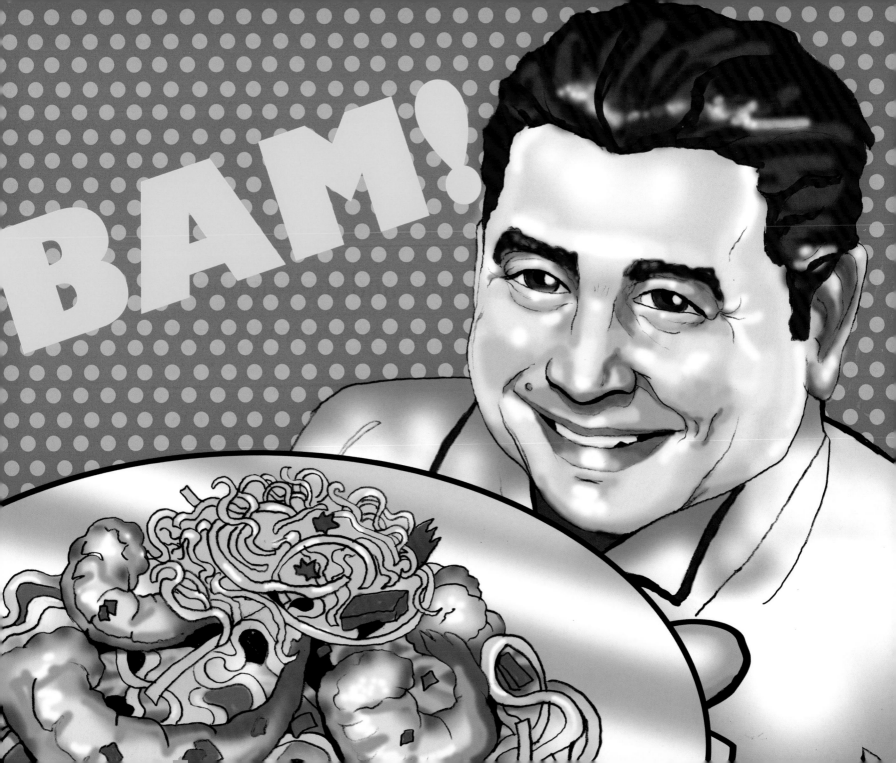

Goodnight to the Aquarium and the Audubon Zoo,
Goodnight to the fishies and animals, too

Goodnight to the Bunny and the bread that he bakes
Goodnight to the Causeway that crosses the Lake

Goodnight doubloons and Mardi Gras things

Goodnight to Rex and to cakes made for Kings

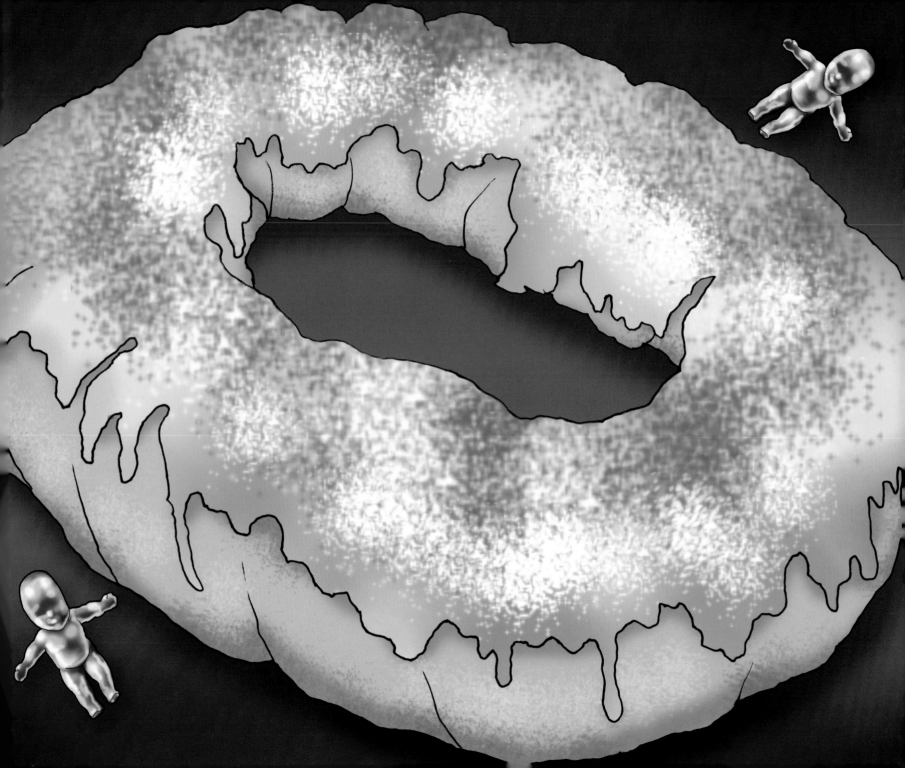

Goodnight to the streetcars and rides which are breezy

Goodnight to the city they call
The Big Easy

ACKNOWLEDGMENTS

We are grateful that our tribute to New Orleans includes such notable people, places and things, and hope that parents will help their children experience the wonderful products and traditions found only in the Crescent City:

Red Beans and Rice – usually on Mondays
Pralines – authentic Creole delicacies
Zatarain's® - the authority on New Orleans spiciness since 1889
The St. Louis Cathedral – built in 1720, the oldest in North America
The French Quarter – founded 1718
Café Du Monde® – in the French Market since 1862
The Mississippi River – second only to the Missouri in length
Po'Boys – since the 1920s (it's all about the bread)
Hubig's Pies – family owned since 1922
Lucky Dogs® – over 21 million sold in the last 50 years
Cooter Brown's – famous fries and beers for famous people

The Louisiana Superdome – largest fixed dome structure in the world
The New Orleans Saints – 1967
The New Orleans Pelicans – 2013
New Orleans Jazz, Blues and Funk – unparalleled
Chef Emeril Lagasse – owner of Emeril's, Del Monico and Nola
Audubon Aquarium of the Americas – home of "Spots," the white alligator
The Audubon Zoo – among the tops in the nation
Bunny Bread – "That's What I Said!"
The Causeway Bridge – longest in the U.S.
Rex, King of Carnival – "Pro Bono Publico" – for the public good since 1872
New Orleans Streetcars – the oldest continuously operating in the world
The Big Easy – named by musicians in the early 1920s